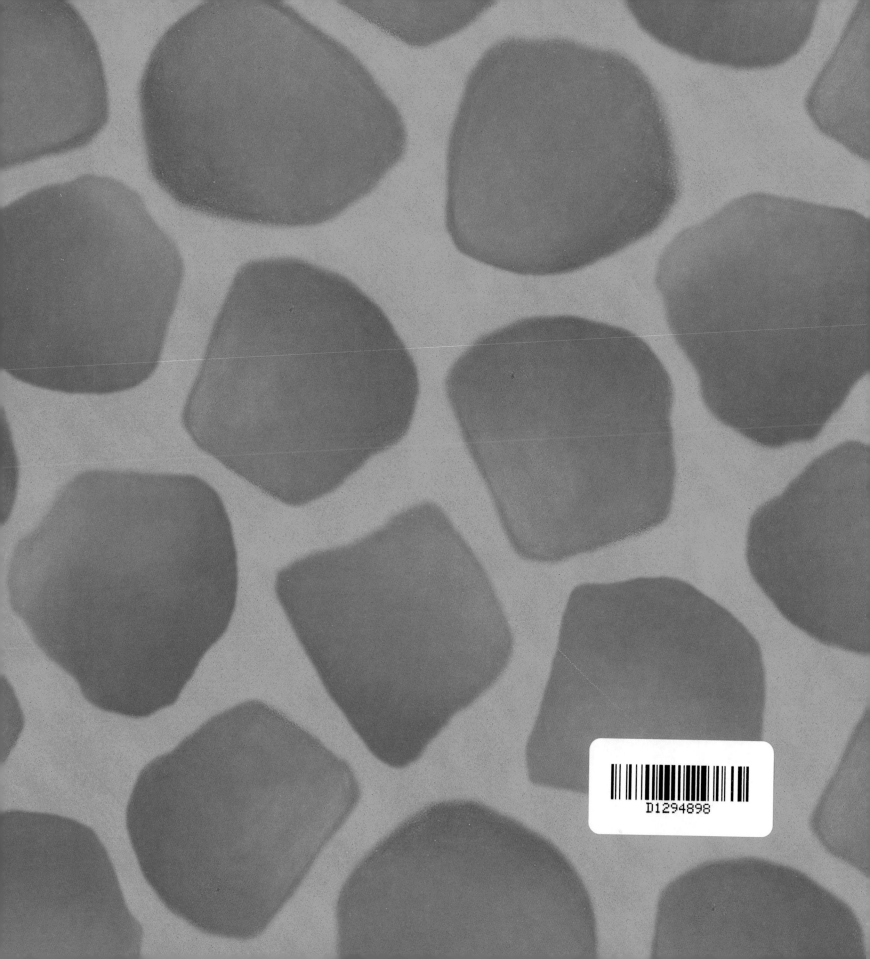

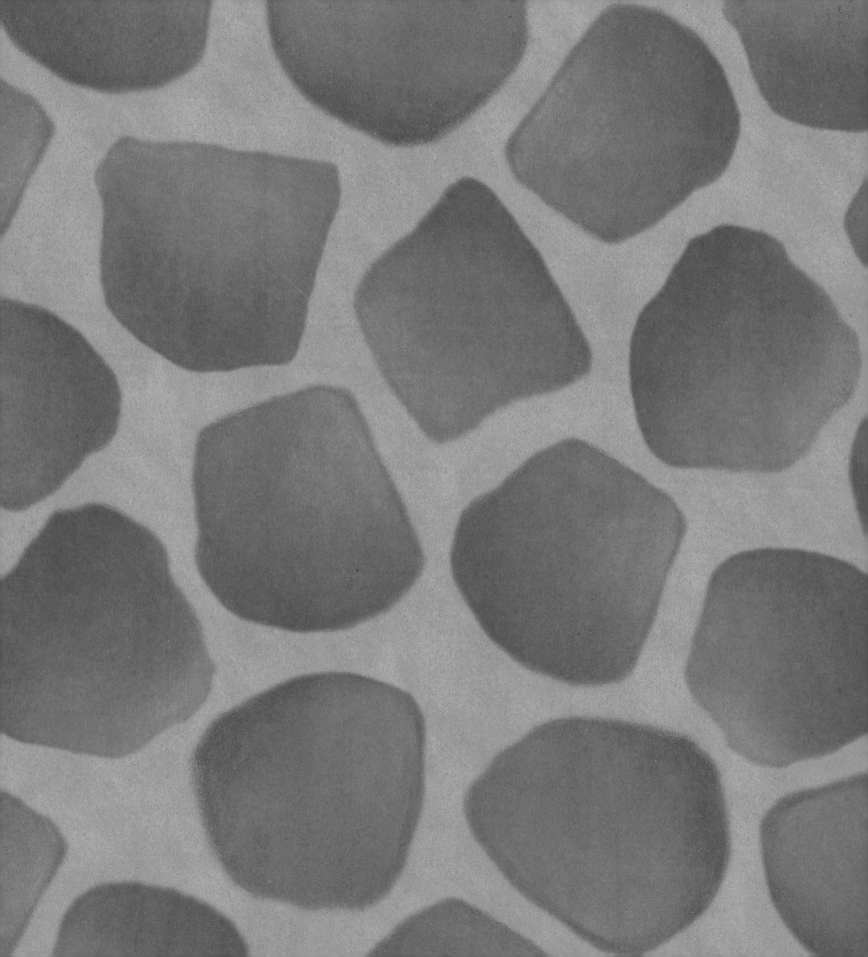

Gilda and Friends

Lucky

An orphan leopard
cub who has the
worst luck

Pepin

A persistent
penguin who loves
his family

Marvin

A silly little
marmoset who is
afraid of heights

Ernest

A young elephant who is
very afraid of mice

Gilda

A friendly giraffe who
loves melons and parties

Zander

A caring,
wise zebra who looks
out for his friends

Leonardo

An adventurous little
lion cub who likes to
go exploring

Papaya

A lovable panda who
eats a lot of bamboo

Turnip

A spirited young
turtle who loves an
adventure

We hope you enjoy the many adventures of Gilda and Friends. Our goal was to maintain the spirit of the original French-language story while adapting it to the Picture Window Books' format. Thank you to the original publisher, author, and illustrator for allowing Picture Window Books to make this series available to a new audience.

Editor: Jacqueline A. Wolfe
Page Production: Tracy Kaehler
Creative Director: Keith Griffin
Editorial Director: Carol Jones
Managing Editor: Catherine Neitge

First American edition published in 2006 by
Picture Window Books
5115 Excelsior Boulevard
Suite 232
Minneapolis, MN 55416
877-845-8392
www.picturewindowbooks.com

First published in Canada in 2000 by
Les éditions Héritage inc.
300 Arran Street
Saint Lambert, Quebec
Canada J4R 1K5

Printed in the United States of America.

Library of Congress Cataloging-in-Publication Data
Papineau, Lucie.
Gilda the giraffe and leonardo the lion cub/ by Lucie Papineau ; illustrated by Marisol Sarrazin.
p. cm. "Gilda the giraffe."
Summary: Bored with his babysitter, Gilda the giraffe, Leonardo the lion cub makes friends with a turtle who
introduces him to the wonders of the ocean, along with a few watery surprises.
ISBN 1-4048-1294-6 (hardcover)
[1. Lions—Fiction. 2. Animals—Fiction. 3. Ocean—Fiction.] I. Sarrazin, Marisol, 1965—ill. II. Title.
PZ7.P2115Gikh 2005
[E]—dc22   2005011294

Gilda the Giraffe

and

Leonardo the Lion Cub

by Lucie Papineau
illustrated by Marisol Sarrazin
story adapted by Michael Dahl

PICTURE WINDOW BOOKS
Minneapolis, Minnesota

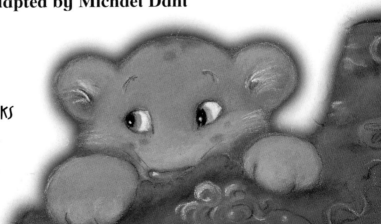

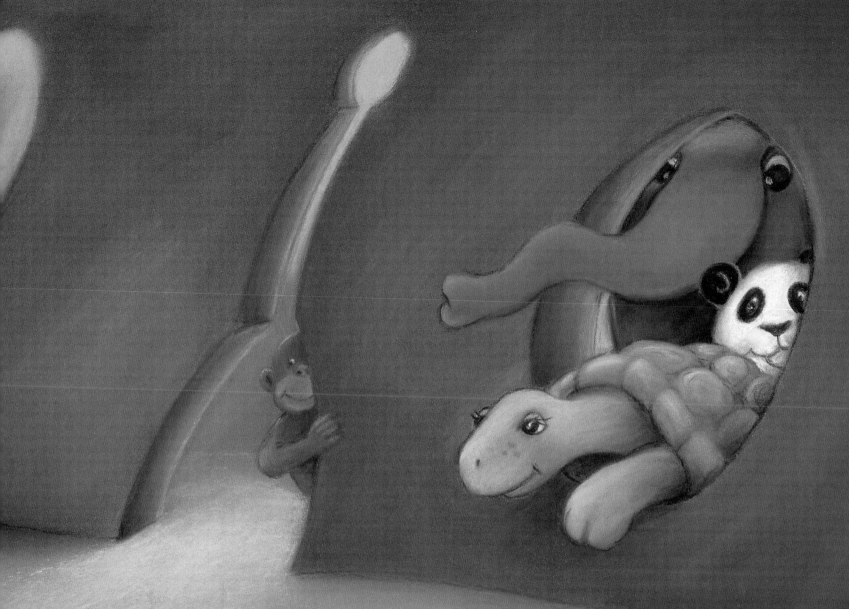

Leonardo the lion cub was visiting
his Aunt Gilda in the jungle. His parents had gone
on a long trip without him. Leonardo liked his aunt, but
he was sad. He missed his family and his friends.
He wanted to go back home.

One morning, Aunt Gilda's doorbell rang.
Some of her friends had stopped by to
meet Leonardo.

Turnip the turtle liked to play. She spun around on her shiny, hard shell. She made funny noises. She picked up one of Aunt Gilda's socks and made a silly face with it.

Leonardo laughed.

"Let's go outside and play," said Leonardo. "Let's go run and jump and growl!"

"Turtles don't growl," said Ernest the elephant. "And Turnip never runs."

"Never?" asked Leonardo.

Turnip shook her head. "But I can do something even better!" she said. "Come outside and see!"

Turnip led Leonardo out of Aunt Gilda's house, through a forest of golden trees, and down to a bright and sunny shore.

"This is where I like to play," said Turnip.

"Down there?" asked Leonardo.

"I may not be able to run," said Turnip, "but I can swim. It's easy. I'll show you how."

Turnip showed Leonardo how to swim through forests of silky seaweed and coral.

Leonardo and his new friend swam deeper under the water. They raced with a herd of seahorses while the lobsters watched and cheered.

15

From out of nowhere, what looked
like a sea serpent charged at
Leonardo. He quickly hid behind a
clump of coral.

Turnip laughed. "That's my little friend. She's not a sea serpent. She just likes to wear a costume and make silly faces."

Turnip decided to take Leonardo for a ride.

They went soaring above the beautiful green sea on the backs of some friendly flying fish.

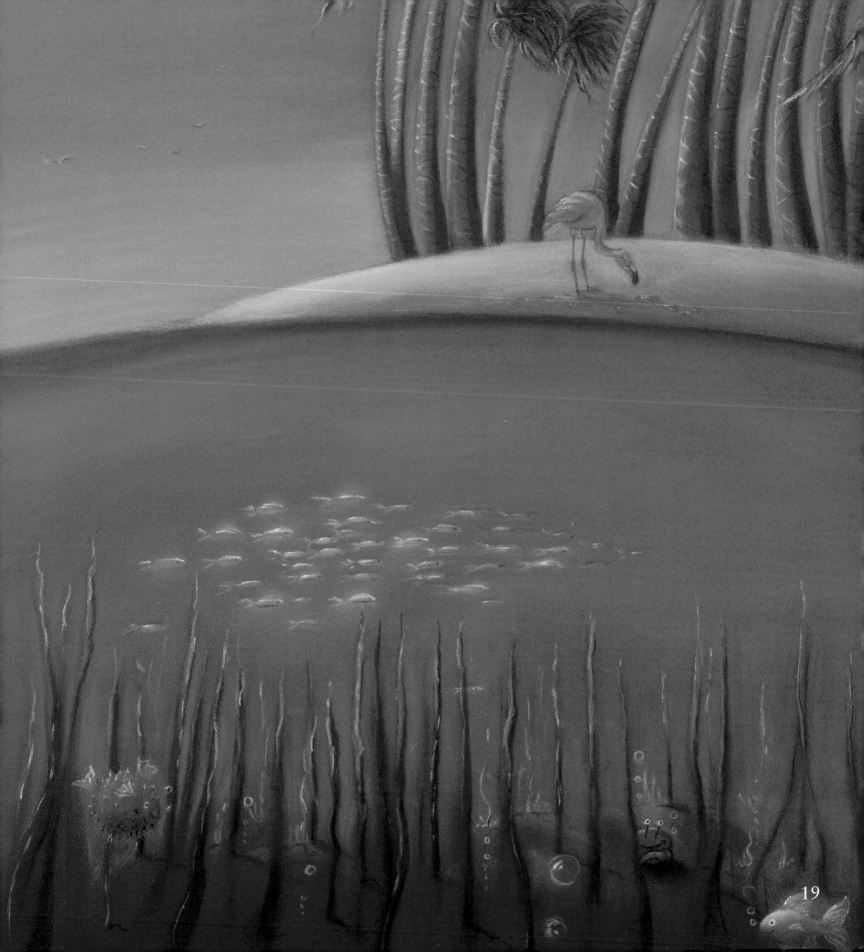

19

Back under the waves, Leonardo and Turnip looked at the radiant starfish.

A moonfish bubbled by, singing a sweet and silly song.

Later, the two new friends floated on their backs and stared up at the violet sky. They watched the stars light up the sky one by one.

"This is much better than running and growling," whispered Leonardo.

Meanwhile, Aunt Gilda was getting worried. It was nighttime, and Leonardo had not come back.

"Don't worry," her friends told her. "We know where Turnip likes to play."

Ernest led the way to the beach.

Down by the shore, the elephant stuck his trunk into the warm, dark water.

He sent out a deep, deep bellow that echoed through the sea. All the fish went to find the lion cub and the turtle.

"I hear
something,"
said Turnip. "It must
be time to go home."

With the help of the lantern
fish, who lit the way, Turnip and
Leonardo swam back to the shore.

Aunt Gilda and her friends were so happy! That night, the sky above the sea blossomed with starry fireworks.

Leonardo thought for a moment. "This is a great place to stay while my parents are away," he said to his new friends.

Fun facts about Gilda's friends ...

- In nature, lions live in the grasslands of Africa.

- A lion can run up to 35 miles (56 kilometers) per hour.

- When an adult lion roars, you can hear it up to 5 miles (8 km) away.

- Sea turtles are strong swimmers and underwater divers. Some can swim as fast as 30 miles (48 km) per hour.

- Sea turtles use their front flippers to help them glide through the water. Their rear flippers help them steer.

Go on more adventures with Gilda the Giraffe:

Gilda the Giraffe and Lucky the Leopard
Gilda the Giraffe and Marvin the Marmoset
Gilda the Giraffe and Papaya the Panda
Gilda the Giraffe and Pepin the Penguin
No More Melons for Gilda the Giraffe
No Spots for Gilda the Giraffe!

On the Web

FactHound offers a safe, fun way to find Internet sites related to this book. All of the sites on FactHound have been researched by our staff.

Here's how:

1. Visit www.facthound.com

2. Type in this special code for age-appropriate sites: 1404812946

3. Click on the FETCH IT button.

Your trusty FactHound will fetch the best sites for you!

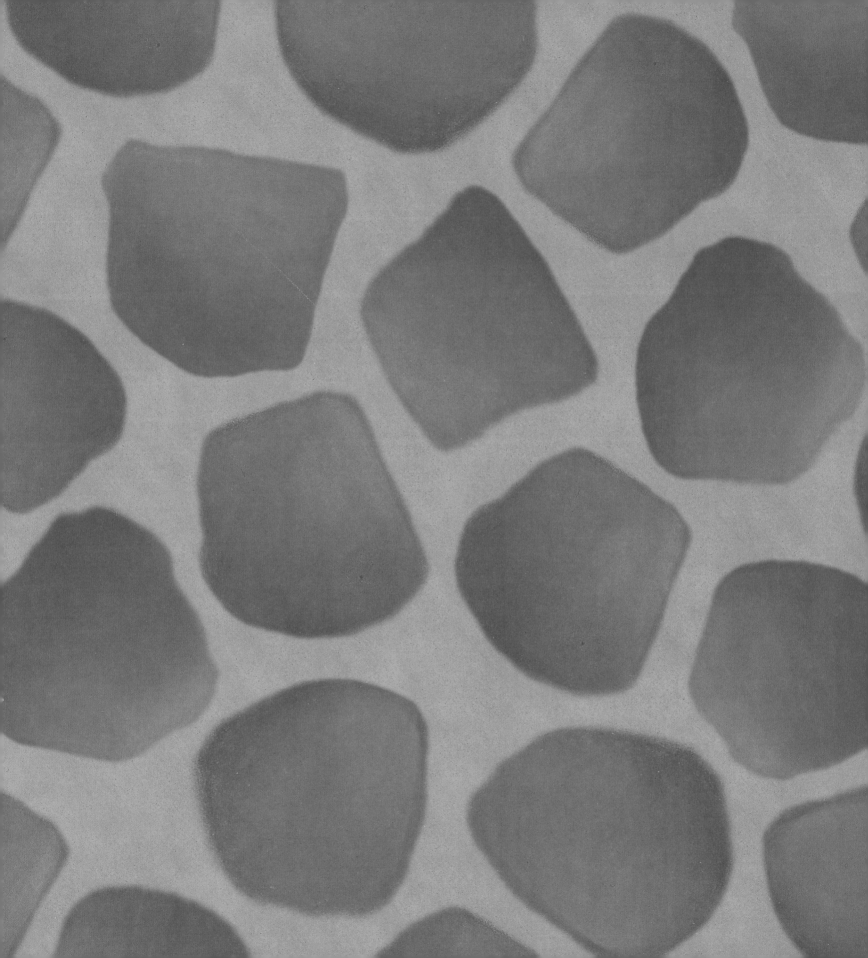